MY 1ST GRAPHIC NOVEL

GOALKEEPER GOOF

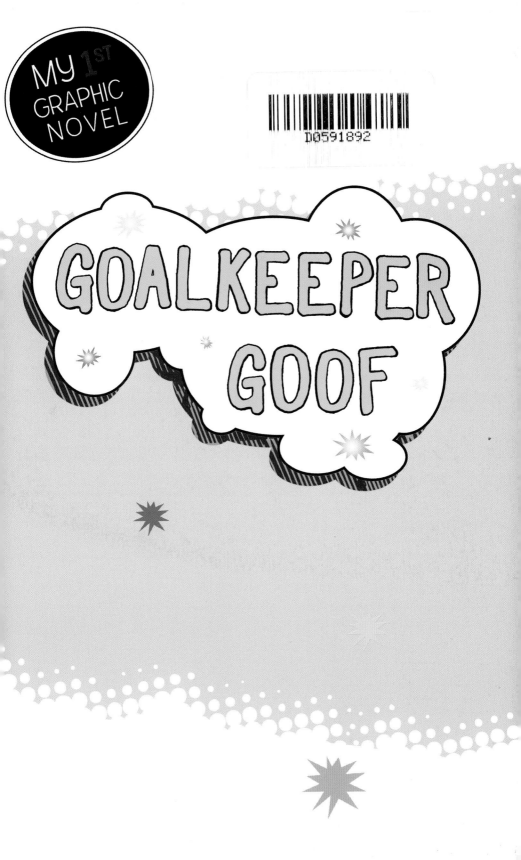

My First Graphic Novels are published by Stone Arch Books,
A Capstone Imprint
1710 Roe Crest Drive
North Mankato, Minnesota 56003
www.capstonepub.com

Library of Congress Cataloging-in-Publication Data
Meister, Cari, 1955-
  Goalkeeper Goof / by Cari Meister; illustrated by Cori Doerrfeld.
  p. cm. — (My first graphic novel)
  ISBN 978-1-4342-1292-4 (library binding)
  ISBN 978-1-4342-1409-6 (pbk.)
  1. Graphic novels. [1. Graphic novels. 2. Soccer—Fiction.] I. Doerrfeld, Cori, ill.
I. Sullivan, Mary, 1958- ill. II. Title.
PZ7.7.M45Go 2009
741.5'973—dc22   2008031965

Summary: David likes soccer, but he doesn't like being goalie. When it's his
turn at the net, he tries a new trick. David is ready to even the score!

Art Director: Heather Kindseth
Graphic Designer: Hilary Wacholz

Printed in the United States of America in Stevens Point, Wisconsin.
022013
007180R

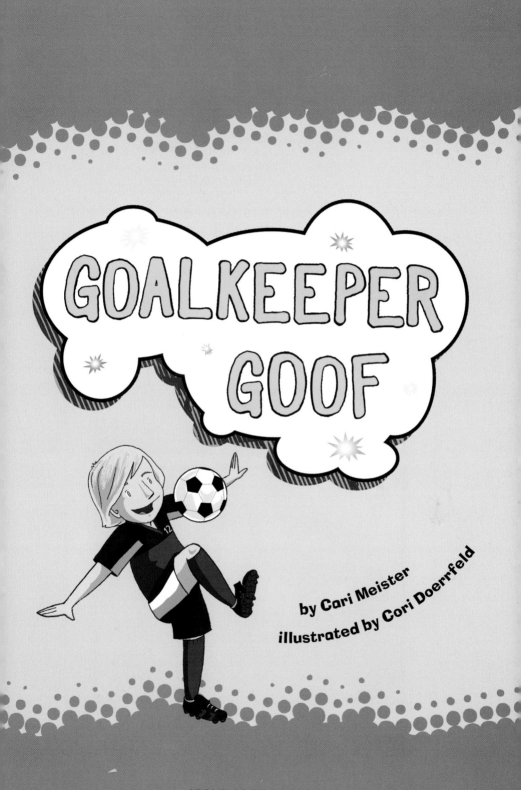

GOALKEEPER GOOF

by Cari Meister

illustrated by Cori Doerrfeld

STONE ARCH BOOKS
www.stonearchbooks.com

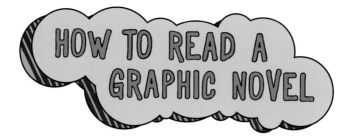

HOW TO READ A GRAPHIC NOVEL

Graphic novels are easy to read. Boxes called panels show you how to follow the story. Look at the panels from left to right and top to bottom.

Read the word boxes and word balloons from left to right as well. Don't forget the sound and action words in the pictures.

The pictures and the words work together to tell the whole story.

David pulled on his shin guards.

He tied the laces on his new cleats.

David frowned. He did not want to go to the soccer game.

At the field, David's team warmed up.

They ran laps.

They dribbled the ball.

Good one!

They kicked the ball.

9

David liked to run. He liked to dribble. He liked to kick.

David was good at those activities.

David did not like to play goalkeeper. He always missed the ball. The other team always scored.

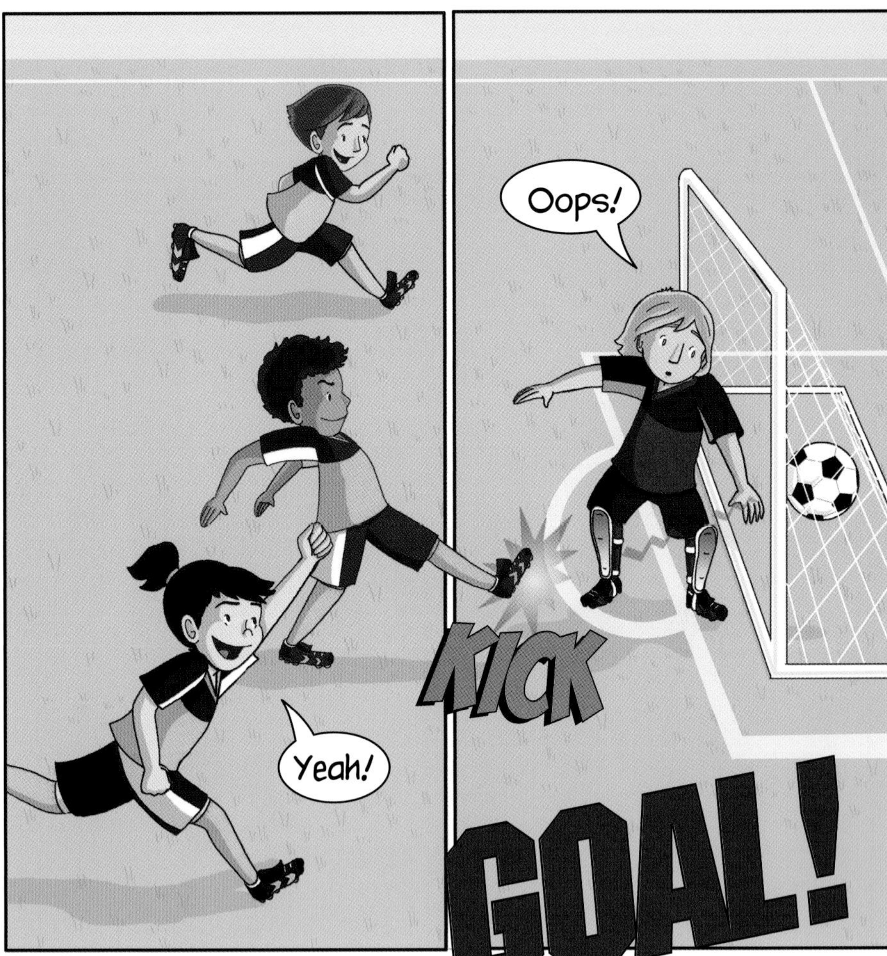
Yeah!
Oops!
KICK
GOAL!

David's team called him the "Goalkeeper Goof."

The first half of the game was great.
David did not play goalkeeper.

He ran.

He dribbled.

He passed the ball to Angel.

Angel scored!

SMACK!

Then David stole the ball.

He kicked.

He scored!

At halftime, the coach talked to the team.

It's your turn to be the goalkeeper, David.

"Keep your eye on the ball," she said. "Don't forget to use your hands."

David always forgot the part about using his hands. Then he had an idea.

David wiggled his fingers.

He ran to the goal. He
kept wiggling his fingers.

"It's the Goalkeeper Goof,"
said Angel.

David pretended not to hear.
He just kept wiggling his fingers.

David watched
the ball.

Here it
comes!

David wiggled his fingers. He was not going to forget to use his hands this time.

The ball was coming right at him! He put up his hands. Then he jumped as high as he could.

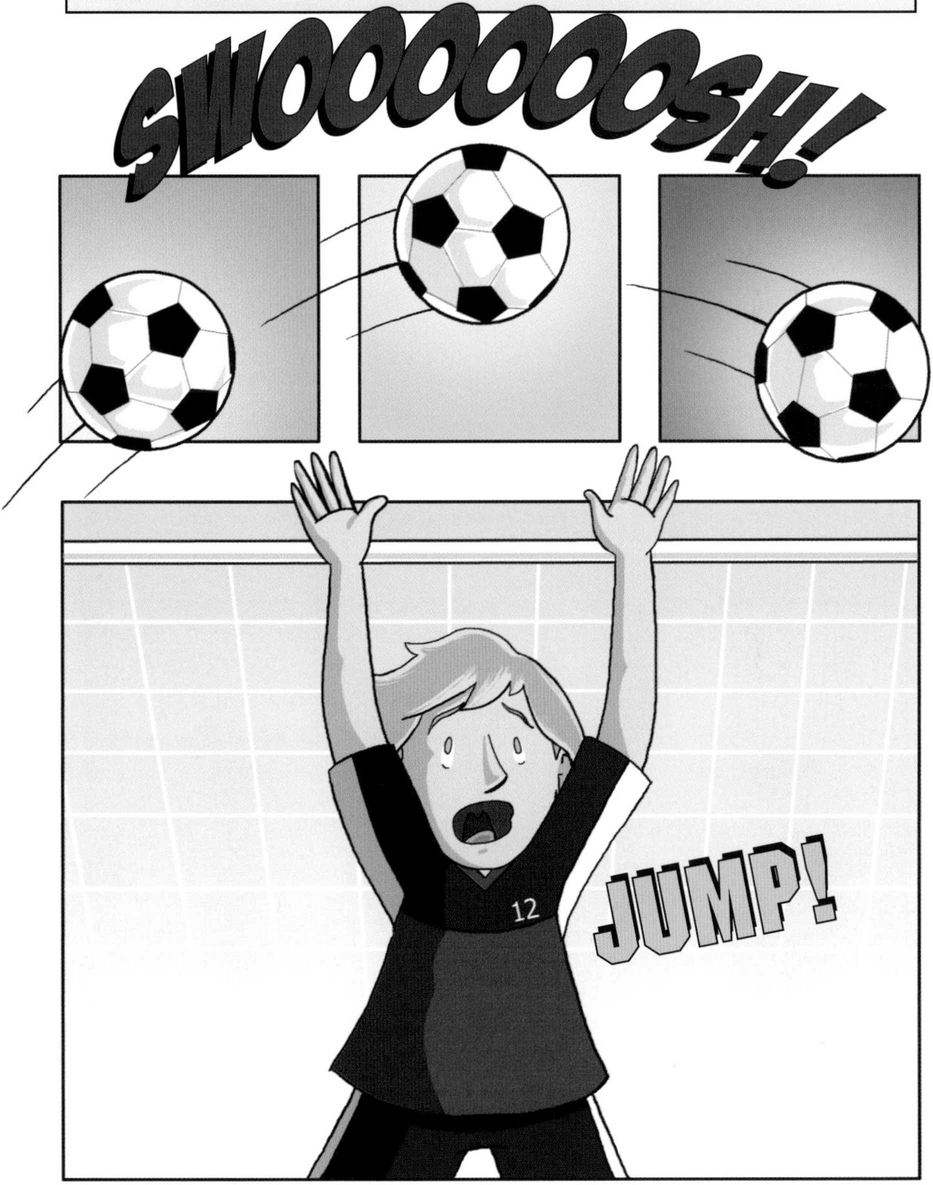
SWOOOOOOSH!
12
JUMP!

He caught the ball!
The game was over.

David was no longer the Goalkeeper Goof! He was the Goalkeeper Champ!

The End

ABOUT THE AUTHOR

Cari Meister is the author of many books for children, including the My Pony Jack series and *Luther's Halloween*. She lives on a small farm in Minnesota with her husband, four sons, three horses, one dog, and one cat. Cari enjoys running, snowshoeing, horseback riding, and yoga. She loves to visit libraries and schools.

ABOUT THE ILLUSTRATOR

Cori Doerrfeld has been drawing since she was a little girl. She always knew she would grow up to be an artist. After studying art and illustration in college, she began work as a children's book illustrator. Cori has illustrated several titles, including a picture book with actress Brooke Shields. When not hard at work painting, Cori enjoys spending time with her daughter, reading comics, and spending time outdoors.

GLOSSARY

cleats (kleetz)—shoes with spikes on the bottom

dribbled (DRIB-uhld)—to move a soccer ball forward by kicking it

goalkeeper (GOHL-keep-ur)—the player who defends the goal

halftime (HAF-time)—the break in the middle of the game

shin guard (shin gard)—a piece of sports equipment that protects the shins

DISCUSSION QUESTIONS

1.) David did not like being teased. Have you ever been teased? If so, what did you do about it?

2.) David's coach believed in him. She knew he would be a good goalkeeper if he kept trying. Have you ever had a coach or a teacher help you with something? If so, what was it?

3.) David thinks of a special trick to help him remember to use his hands. Have you ever used a trick to remember something?

1.) If you were the coach, what kind of
warm-up would you create? Write down
at least three warm-up activities. Then
grab some friends and try them out.

2.) In the book, David has two nicknames.
Write down some friendly nicknames
for your friends and family.

3.) Throughout the book, there are sound and
action words next to some of the art. Pick at
least two of those words. Then write your own
sentences using those words.

THE FIRST STEP INTO GRAPHIC NOVELS

MY 1st GRAPHIC NOVEL

THE KICKBALL KIDS

by Cari Meister
Illustrated by Julie Olson

SPORTS FICTION

MY 1st GRAPHIC NOVEL

LILY'S LUCKY LEOTARD

by Cari Meister
Illustrated by Jannie Ho

My FIRST Graphic Novel

These books are the perfect introduction to the world of safe, appealing graphic novels. Each story uses familiar topics, repeating patterns, and core vocabulary words appropriate for a beginning reader. Combine the entertaining story with comic book panels, exciting action elements, and bright colors and a safe graphic novel is born.

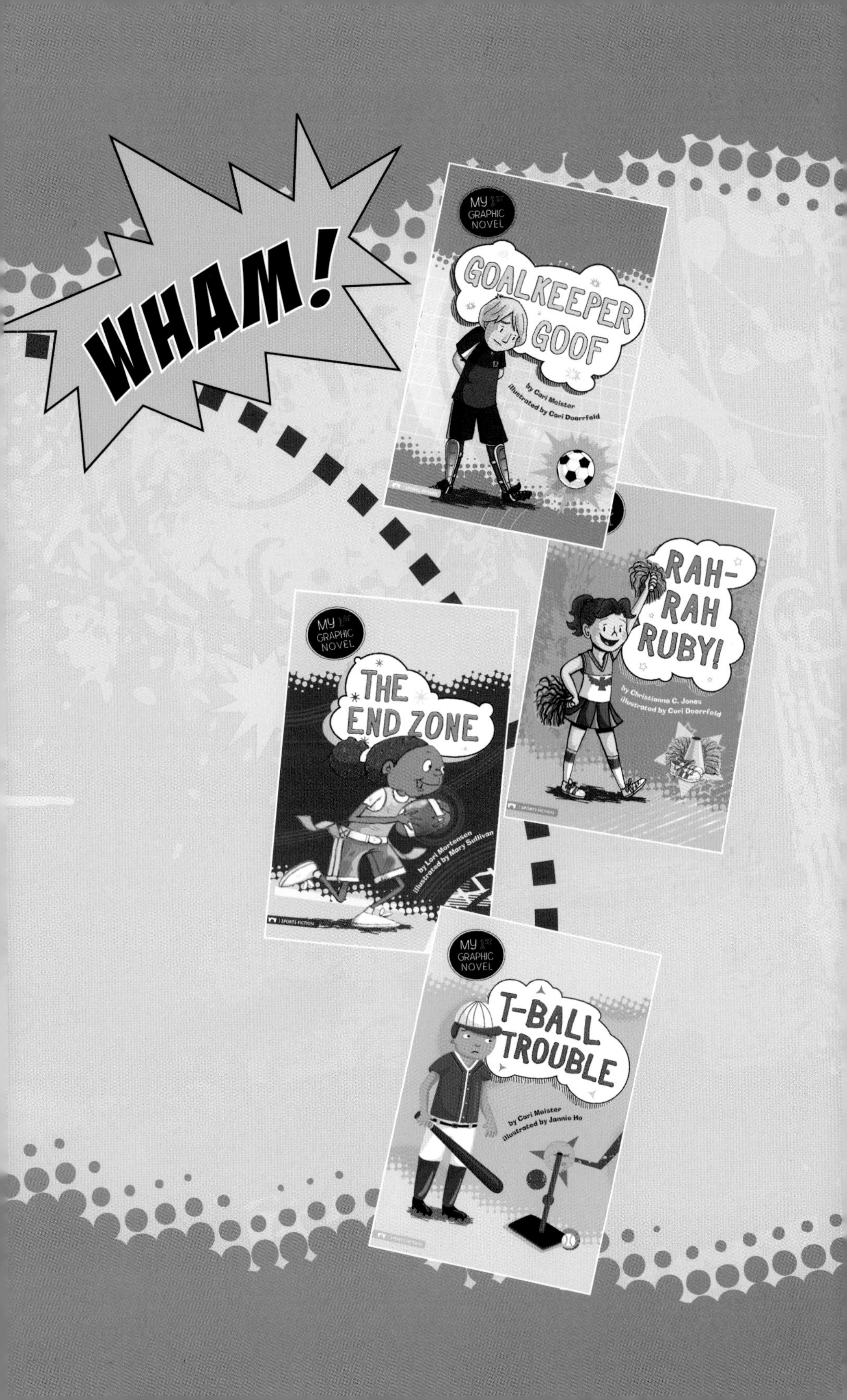
WHAM!
MY 1ST GRAPHIC NOVEL
GOALKEEPER GOOF
by Cari Meister
illustrated by Cori Doerrfeld
RAH-RAH RUBY!
by Christianne C. Jones
illustrated by Cori Doerrfeld
MY 1ST GRAPHIC NOVEL
THE END ZONE
by Lori Mortensen
illustrated by Mary Sullivan
SPORTS FICTION
MY 1ST GRAPHIC NOVEL
T-BALL TROUBLE
by Cari Meister
illustrated by Jannie Ho